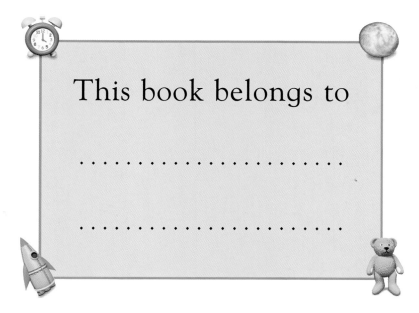

This book belongs to

. . . .

. . . .

LONDON, NEW YORK, SYDNEY, PARIS, MUNICH, and JOHANNESBURG

Written in consultation with child psychologist
Flora Hogman, Ph.D.

Project Editor Hannah Wilson
Senior Art Editor Sonia Whillock
Senior Editor Linda Esposito
U.S. Editor Beth Sutinis
Production Chris Avgherinos and Silvia La Greca
Jacket Design Karen Shooter

First American Edition, 2001
Published in the United States by DK Publishing, Inc.
375 Hudson Street, New York, NY 10014

2 4 6 8 10 9 7 5 3 1

Library of Congress Cataloging-in-Publication Data

Robbins, Beth.
    Tom's afraid of the dark! / by Beth Robbins ; illustrated by Jon Stuart.-- 1st American ed.
        p. cm. -- (It's O.K.)
    Summary: Tom, a young cat, overcomes his fear of the dark by using his imagination to
    think about good things rather than bad ones.
    ISBN 0-7894-7421-2 -- ISBN 0-7894-7420-4 (pbk.)
    [1. Fear of the dark--Fiction. 2. Bedtime--Fiction. 3. Imagination--Fiction. 4. Cats--Fiction.]
    I. Stuart, Jon, ill. II. Title. III. Series.

PZ7.R53235 To 2001
[E]--dc21   2001028160

Color reproduction by Colourscan, Singapore
Printed and bound by L.E.G.O. in Italy

see our complete
catalog at
www.dk.com

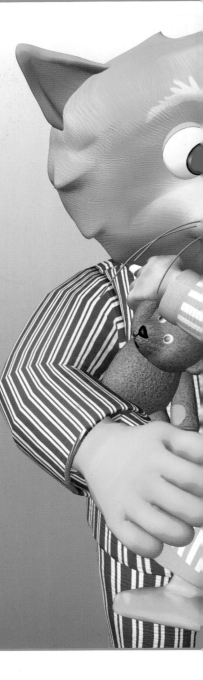

IT'S OK!

TOM'S AFRAID OF THE DARK!

BY BETH ROBBINS

ILLUSTRATED BY JON STUART

DK Publishing, Inc.

"O.K., kittens, it's time for bed," said Mom.
"Look at the time."

Ally made a face.

"I don't want to go to bed,"
meowed Tom.

"All right," said Mom.
"Five more minutes."

Tom and Ally raced to the toy box.

They pulled out every single toy.

"I'm King Tom!"

"We're having
a birthday party!
Who wants some cake?"

6

"Ship ahoy! I'm a pirate!"

"Ladies and gentlemen, please welcome Ally the magician!"

"Hi, fans! I'm going to sing my latest song!"

"What amazing imaginations they have!" said Dad.

"Your five minutes are up!" said Mom.
"Let's pick up these toys, and then it's time for bed."

"Why don't grown-ups have to go to bed early?" meowed Ally.
"Kittens need more sleep than grown-ups,"
replied Mom.
"Why?" asked Tom.

"So they grow healthy
and strong," said Dad.

"Look," said Dad.
"Even the sun's going to bed."

Tom and Ally watched
the sun disappear.

"Soon it will be dark,"
whispered Tom.

Ally and Tom got ready for bed.

Tom put
on his pajamas.

Ally put on
her pajamas.

Ally brushed her teeth.

Tom brushed his teeth.

Tom washed his face.

Ally washed her face.

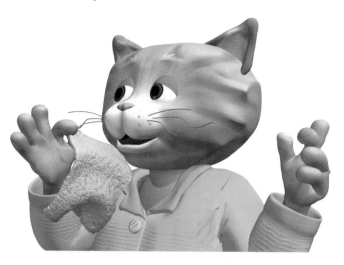

Ally combed her whiskers . . . but Tom didn't!

Dad and the kittens sat on Ally's bed.
"What kind of story should we read?" he asked.

"I like monster stories!" cried Ally.
Dad picked out a monster story and began to read aloud.

Tom didn't want to say anything,
but he thought monster stories were a little scary.

When Dad finished the story,
Ally climbed onto her chair.
"I'm a hairy monster!" she cried.

Then she made a monster face
and waved her arms around.

"Get off the chair, Ally," said Dad.

"Are there really monsters?"
asked Tom.

Dad gave him a hug.
"Only in your imagination,"
he replied.

13

"What's imagination?" whispered Tom.
But Dad didn't hear him
because Ally was roaring and shouting.

Just then, Mom came into the room.
"Bedtime," she said in a firm voice.

Dad put Ally to bed,
while Mom carried Tom to his room.

Mom tucked Tom into bed.

"Are there *really* monsters?" asked Tom.
"Monsters are only in your imagination,"
said Mom, kissing him good night.

"What's imagination?"
whispered Tom.

But Mom didn't hear him
because Ally was calling
for a glass of milk.

15

Tom lay awake in the dark.
Everything in his room looked strange and scary.

What was that by the door?
It looked just like a monster!
Could there be a monster in his room?

Tom ran into Ally's bedroom and woke her up.
"There's a monster in my room!" he cried.

Ally sat up and rubbed her eyes.
"Don't be silly," she said.
"It's just your imagination."

Ally took Tom back to his room
and switched on the light.

"See!" she said. "There are no monsters!
I told you it was your imagination."

"What's imagination?" asked Tom.
But Ally didn't hear him
because she had already gone back to bed.

Tom closed his eyes, but he still couldn't sleep.

Then out of the darkness came a long growl.
Tom held his breath and listened.
He heard the growl again.

Tom tried hiding under his covers, but it was no good.
He had to find Mom and Dad.

He slid out of bed and tiptoed into the hall.

The growling grew very loud . . . and then very quiet.
It stopped . . . and then started again.
It had to be a monster. But where was it coming from?

Tom pushed open the door
to Mom and Dad's room.
Suddenly the growl turned into a snort.

"Are you awake, too?" asked Dad.
Tom's eyes were wide with fright.
"Where's the growling monster?" he cried.

"That's not a monster,"
chuckled Dad.
"That's Mom snoring!"

He picked up Tom
and carried him
back to bed.

 But Tom couldn't sleep.

First he was too hot.

Then he was too cold.

He tried lying on his front.

He tried lying on his back.

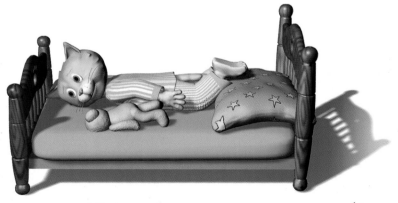

He even tried lying the wrong way around!

Tom climbed out of bed
and looked out the window.
It was very, very dark outside.

He looked around his room.
It was very, very dark inside, too.

Everything everywhere
looked spooky.
Tom began to cry.

"What's the matter?" asked Mom.
"I'm afraid of the dark!" cried Tom.
"It makes everything spooky!"

"The dark is nothing to be afraid of," said Dad.
"You're only afraid because your imagination
is making you think of scary things."
"If you think of happy things, you won't be afraid," said Mom.

Dad wrapped Tom in a blanket.
"I'm going to show you
a secret about the dark," he said.

Dad carried Tom outside.
The moon was shining brightly,
and thousands of stars were twinkling in the sky.

"See," said Dad. "Even the dark is not really dark."

Tom looked around the yard.
Dad was right. The dark wasn't really dark.
And nothing looked spooky or scary at all.

Dad tucked Tom into bed.

"I was afraid of the dark
when I was little," he said.
"Then, one night, my dad
took me outside and showed me
the stars." Dad smiled.
"After that, I was never afraid
of the dark again."

Tom was amazed.
He never thought Dad would be
frightened of anything.

"Mom, what's imagination?"
yawned Tom.

Mom sat down beside him.
"Imagination means thinking up
all kinds of different things," said Mom.
"Nice things as well as nasty things."

Tom thought hard.
"I'm going to think about nice things," he said.
"Then I won't be frightened anymore."

31

Tom lay awake in the dark.
He thought about
being a king.

He thought about
being a pirate.

And he wasn't frightened at all.

Tom rolled over in his bed
and very soon he was fast asleep.